Rosie ᴬɴᴅ Michael

JUDITH VIORST

Illustrated by Lorna Tomei

Aladdin Paperbacks

Aladdin Paperbacks
An imprint of Simon & Schuster
Children's Publishing Division
1230 Avenue of the Americas
New York, NY 10020
Text copyright © 1974 by Judith Viorst
Illustrations copyright © 1974 by Lorna Tomei
First Aladdin Paperbacks edition, 1979
Second Aladdin Paperbacks edition, 1988
Also available in a hardcover edition from Atheneum Books for Young Readers
Manufactured in the United States of America

10   9   8

Library of Congress Cataloging-in-Publication Data
Viorst, Judith.
Rosie and Michael.
Summary: Two friends tell what they like about each other—even the bad things.
[1. Friendship—Fiction]   I. Tomei, Lorna, ill.   II. Title.
[PZ7.V816Ro   1986]   [E]   86-13969
ISBN 0-689-71272-3 (pbk.)

For Sheila King Clarke, a special friend

Rosie is my friend.

She likes me when I'm dopey and not just when I'm smart.

I worry a lot about pythons, and she understands.

My toes point in,
and my shoulders droop,
and there's hair growing
out of my ears.

But Rosie says I look good.

She is my friend.

Michael is my friend.

He likes me when I'm grouchy
and not just when I'm nice.

I worry a lot about were-
wolves, and he understands.
There's freckles growing all
over me, except on my eye-
balls and teeth.

But Michael says I look good.

He is my friend.

When I said that my nickname was Mickey, Rosie said Mickey. When I said that my nickname was Ace, Rosie said Ace. And when I was Tiger, and Lefty, and Ringo, Rosie always remembered.

That's how friends are.

When I wrote my name with a *y,* Michael wrote Rosey. When I wrote my name with an *i,* Michael wrote Rosi. And when I wrote Rosee, and Rozi, and Wrosie, Michael always did too.

That's how friends are.

Just because I sprayed Kool Whip in her sneakers,
doesn't mean that Rosie's not my friend.

Just because I let the air out of his basketball, doesn't mean that Michael's not my friend.

1/14/98

Mrs. Belcher

I tried to help Jonathan with his homework and I did not understand the directions. (pages 52-53) Could you take a moment and explain the directions to Jonathan and I will be happy to see that it is finished.

Thank you
Karen

When my parakeet died, I called Rosie.

When my bike got swiped, I called Rosie.

When I cut my head and the blood came
gushing out, as soon as the blood stopped
gushing, I called Rosie.

She is my friend.

When my dog ran away,
I called Michael. When my bike got swiped,
I called Michael. When I broke my wrist
and the bone was sticking out,
as soon as they stuck it back in,
I called Michael.

He is my friend.

It wouldn't matter if two billion people said she robbed a bank.

If Rosie told me she didn't, I'd believe her.

Even though his fingerprints were found all over the dagger, if Michael said, "I'm innocent," I'd believe him.

Just because I dug a
hole and covered it with

leaves and told her to
jump on the leaves

and she fell in the hole, doesn't mean that Rosie's not my friend.

Just because I put a worm in his tuna salad sandwich,
doesn't mean that Michael's not my friend.

Rosie is my friend. I sold her my yo-yo that glows in
the dark for only fifty cents. I would have charged
Alvin Alpert seventy-five.

Michael is my friend. I traded him my whiffle bat for
only fourteen marbles. It would have been twenty
marbles for Alvin Alpert.

If Rosie told me a
secret and people hit
me and bit me, I
wouldn't tell what
Rosie's secret was. And
then if people twisted
my arm and kicked me
in the shins, I still
wouldn't tell what
Rosie's secret was. And
then if people said,
"Speak up, or we'll
throw you in this quick-
sand," Rosie would
forgive me for telling
her secret.

If Michael told me a secret and people clonked me and bopped me, I wouldn't tell what Michael's secret was. And then if people bent back my fingers and wrestled me to the ground, I still wouldn't tell what Michael's secret was.

And then if people said, "Speak up, or we'll feed you to these piranhas," Michael would forgive me for telling his secret.

Just because I call her a

GORILLA

FACE

doesn't mean that
Rosie's not my friend.

Just because I call him a

doesn't mean that
Michael's not my friend.

Sometimes I get on the diving board and decide that
I've changed my mind. But Rosie wouldn't laugh.
She is my friend.

Sometimes I'm climbing up a tree and decide that
I'd rather climb down. But Michael wouldn't laugh.
He is my friend.

If Rosie bought me an ice-cream bar, it wouldn't be toasted almond. If Rosie bought me a shirt, it wouldn't be green. If Rosie bought me a book, it wouldn't be *How Your Sewer System Works,* or *Sven of Sweden.*

You can count on a friend.

If Michael bought me some candy, it wouldn't be licorice. If Michael bought me a scarf, it wouldn't be brown. If Michael bought me a book, it wouldn't be *Know Your Lungs,* or *Dances of Costa Rica.*

You can count on a friend.

Even though I was voted Most Horrible Singing Voice
in the Class, Rosie says that Alvin Alpert sings worse.

Even though I was voted Bossiest Person in the Class,
Michael says that Alvin Alpert is bossier.

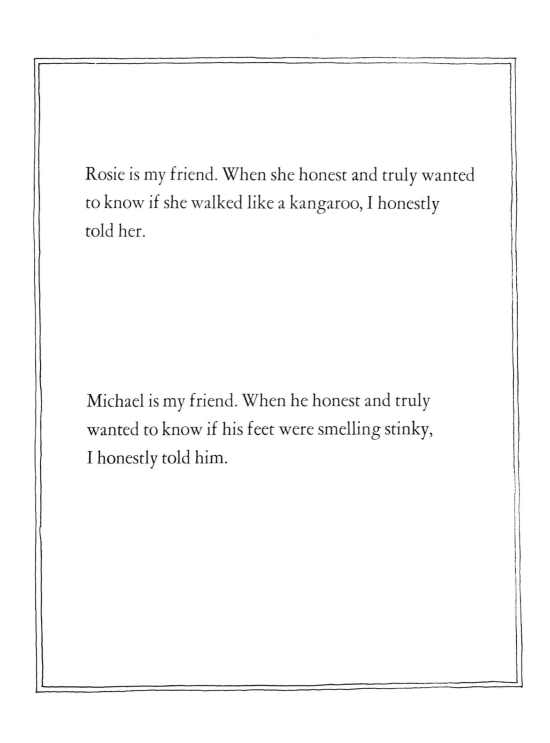

Rosie is my friend. When she honest and truly wanted to know if she walked like a kangaroo, I honestly told her.

Michael is my friend. When he honest and truly wanted to know if his feet were smelling stinky, I honestly told him.

Rosie would try to save me if there was a tidal wave.

She'd hunt for me if kidnappers stole me away.

And if I never was found again, she could have my Instamatic. She is my friend.

Michael would try to save me
if a lion attacked.

He'd catch me if I jumped
from a burning house.

And if by mistake he missed the catch, he could have my
stamp collection.   He is my friend.

I'd never get my tonsils out if Rosie didn't, too.

I'd never move to China without Michael.

I'd give her my last piece of chalk.

I'd give him my last Chicklet.

Rosie is

Michael is

My friend.